"Whispered Promises: A R̶̶̶̶ u
Uloaku"

Chapter 1

Chapter 2.

Chapter 3: ̶

Chapter 4: Th̶ ...ng of Secrets

Chapter 5: A Journey to Self-Discovery

Chapter 6: The Power of Forgiveness

Chapter 7: Amidst the Storm

Chapter 8: A Love Tested

Chapter 9: Healing Wounds, Mending Hearts

Chapter 10: Embracing the Unknown

Chapter 11: The Depths of Despair

Chapter 12: A Twist of Fate

Chapter 13: The Strength of True Love

Chapter 14: Redemption and Second Chances

Chapter 15: Forever in Each Other's Arms

"Whispered Promises: A Romantic Tale of Uju Uloaku"

Acknowledgments:

First and foremost, I would like to express my deepest gratitude to my family. Your unwavering support and belief in my abilities have been the pillars upon which this work stands.

To my friends and colleagues, your insightful conversations and challenging questions have been instrumental in shaping this book. Your camaraderie has made this journey enjoyable and fulfilling.

I would also like to extend my thanks to the countless authors and thinkers whose works have inspired and informed my own. Your contributions to the field have paved the way for explorations such as this one.

Lastly, to my readers, thank you for embarking on this journey with me. This book is a labour of love, and I hope it resonates with you as much as it has with me.

"Whispered Promises: A Romantic Tale of Uju Uloaku"

Thank you all for being a part of this incredible journey. This book is as much yours as it is mine. Here's to many more!

"Whispered Promises: A Romantic Tale of Uju Uloaku"

Introduction:

In a world where love often dances on the edge of uncertainty, where hearts yearn for connection and souls crave fulfilment, a story unfolds. "Whispered Promises" is a captivating tale of love, passion, and the resilience of the human spirit, centred around the remarkable journey of Uju Uloaku.

Uju, a vibrant and ambitious young woman, finds herself at the crossroads of life's unpredictable maze. Set against the backdrop of a bustling city, her story begins with a chance encounter that sets her heart ablaze and ignites a fire within her that cannot be contained. As the rain falls softly, creating a symphony of hope, destiny steps in, intertwining her path with that of an enigmatic stranger.

Chapter by chapter, this poignant narrative will guide you through the twists and turns of Uju's extraordinary journey. From the exhilarating moments of falling in love to the arduous trials that threaten to tear them apart, you will witness the depth of human emotions and the complexities of relationships. Each chapter reveals a new layer, weaving a tale of passion, sacrifice, and the triumph of love.

In the first chapter, "A Chance Encounter," Uju stumbles upon a charming stranger named Chinedu during a crowded street festival. As their eyes lock, time seems to stand still, and their destinies become intertwined. The following chapter, "Love Blossoms in the Rain," explores the magical moments when Uju and Chinedu delve deeper into their connection, their hearts opening to the possibility of a love that transcends all boundaries.

However, their journey is not without challenges. In "Trials and Tribulations," Uju and Chinedu face obstacles that test the strength of their bond. Secrets are unveiled in "The Unveiling of Secrets," and Uju is confronted with the truth that threatens to shatter her world. Through "A Journey to Self-Discovery," Uju embarks on a path of introspection, seeking answers and finding the resilience to confront her past.

"Whispered Promises: A Romantic Tale of Uju Uloaku"

As the story progresses, themes of forgiveness, resilience, and the power of love take centre stage. In "The Power of Forgiveness," Uju and Chinedu learn that forgiveness holds the key to their emotional liberation. "Amidst the Storm" delves into the turbulent times when their love is tested, forcing them to confront their deepest fears and insecurities.

While traversing the chapters, you will witness the transformative power of love in "Healing Wounds, Mending Hearts." Uju and Chinedu navigate the delicate process of healing, as they both strive to overcome the scars of their pasts. Their shared journey becomes a testament to the redemptive nature of love and its ability to conquer even the most profound pain.

Through the chapters that follow, Uju and Chinedu embrace the unknown, face the depths of despair, and experience unexpected twists of fate. It is in these moments of vulnerability and uncertainty that their love shines brightest, ultimately leading them to the culmination of their emotional odyssey.

"Whispered Promises: A Romantic Tale of Uju Uloaku"

"Whispered Promises: A Romantic Tale of Uju Uloaku" is an exploration of the human heart, a celebration of love's triumph over adversity, and a reminder that true love is worth fighting for. Prepare to be captivated by a tale that will transport you to the depths of passion, the heights of emotion, and the profound beauty of two souls intertwined in a love that defies all odds.

"Whispered Promises: A Romantic Tale of Uju Uloaku"

Chapter 1: A Chance Encounter

The city streets hummed with life as Uju Uloaku meandered through the crowd. It was the annual street festival, a kaleidoscope of colours and sounds that filled the air with an intoxicating energy. Uju had always been drawn to the vibrancy of the city, its pulsating heartbeat echoing her own desire for adventure and connection.

As she navigated through the maze of people, her eyes fell upon a captivating sight. A young man stood on a makeshift stage, his voice carrying through the air like an enchanting melody. Uju found herself transfixed; her gaze fixed upon him as if caught in a trance.

The stranger's voice resonated with an inexplicable familiarity, as if it held a secret connection to the deepest recesses of her soul. Her heart quickened its pace, each beat echoing the cadence of the music that swirled around them. Uju was drawn to him, captivated by the raw passion that emanated from his very being.

"Whispered Promises: A Romantic Tale of Uju Uloaku"

As the song reached its crescendo, the crowd erupted in applause, their cheers merging with the distant sound of raindrops gently cascading from the heavens. The sky had opened, casting a soft veil upon the city. Uju, her heart racing with anticipation, felt an irresistible pull, as if some invisible force beckoned her to the stranger on stage.

She took hesitant steps towards him, the rain enveloping her like a cloak of possibility. Her eyes met his, and for a fleeting moment, time ceased to exist. It was as if the universe had conspired to bring them together, their connection written in the stars.

Uju found herself standing at the edge of the stage, her gaze locked with his. In that instant, the world around them faded away, leaving only the two of them in an intimate dance of destiny. His eyes held a depth that mirrored her own longing, and she could sense the unspoken promises whispered between their souls.

As the last notes of the song lingered in the air, he stepped down from the stage, extending his hand towards her. Uju, her heart ablaze with a newfound courage, reached out and clasped his hand, surrendering to the pull of fate.

They stood there, their hands intertwined, raindrops gently tracing a path down their faces. It was a moment suspended in time, a moment that held the promise of something extraordinary. Uju knew, deep in her heart, that her life would never be the same again.

Little did she know that this chance encounter was just the beginning of a remarkable journey, one filled with joy and heartache, passion, and sacrifice. Their love story would transcend boundaries, defy societal expectations, and prove that when two souls collide in a moment of destiny, their connection can withstand the tests of time.

As Uju and the stranger walked into the night, their footsteps fading into the distance, the rain whispered its blessings upon their whispered promises. And so, their tale of love, longing, and unyielding devotion began to unfold, leaving an indelible mark on their souls and the

"Whispered Promises: A Romantic Tale of Uju Uloaku"

hearts of those who would come to witness their extraordinary love affair.

Chapter 2: Love Blossoms in the Rain

The rain continued to fall, enveloping the city in a symphony of whispered promises. As Uju and the stranger walked side by side, their hands still intertwined, they found themselves drawn towards the shelter of a nearby cafe. It was as if the rain itself conspired to create a sacred space for their burgeoning love to flourish.

Inside the cozy cafe, the air was thick with the aroma of freshly brewed coffee and the soft murmur of conversations. Uju and the stranger found a secluded corner, a haven within the bustling world outside, where they could delve deeper into their connection.

Their eyes locked, a cascade of emotions passing between them. Uju felt a warmth spread through her being, a comfort she had never known before. It was as if they had known each other for a lifetime, their souls recognizing one another amidst the chaos of the world.

"Whispered Promises: A Romantic Tale of Uju Uloaku"

He introduced himself as Chinedu, his voice a gentle whisper that resonated deep within Uju's heart. She shared her own name, her voice carrying a trace of vulnerability and anticipation. Their conversation flowed effortlessly, as if the words were merely vessels for the unspoken emotions that surged between them.

Time lost its meaning as they exchanged stories, dreams, and fears. Uju discovered that Chinedu was a talented musician, his melodies born from a place of profound passion and introspection. His music became a mirror through which Uju glimpsed the depth of his soul, a soul that resonated with her own longing for expression and connection.

As the rain continued to fall outside, a sense of intimacy blossomed within the walls of the cafe. Uju found herself sharing fragments of her life, her dreams, and her vulnerabilities with Chinedu. It was as if she had found a kindred spirit, someone who understood the depths of her being without needing to speak a word.

Chinedu, too, bared his soul to her, sharing the moments of triumph and heartbreak that had shaped him into the person he was. Uju listened with rapt attention, her heart expanding with each revelation. In those vulnerable moments, they forged a bond that transcended the superficialities of everyday life.

As their connection deepened, Uju and Chinedu discovered a shared passion for the arts, for the power of creativity to heal and uplift. They spoke of their dreams, their aspirations, and the desire to make a difference in the world through their respective talents. It was a meeting of minds, a convergence of dreams that made their love feel like a force of nature, unstoppable and eternal.

Outside, the rain intensified, tapping against the cafe windows as if in applause of the love that was blossoming within. Uju's heart swelled with emotions that threatened to spill over, and she couldn't help but wonder if this was the beginning of something extraordinary.

"Whispered Promises: A Romantic Tale of Uju Uloaku"

Chinedu, sensing her inner turmoil, reached out and gently wiped a tear that escaped down her cheek. His touch was tender, a feather-light caress that sent shivers down Uju's spine. In that moment, she realized that this love, their love, was both a fragile flower and an unyielding oak, capable of weathering any storm.

Their eyes locked once again, and in the depths of Chinedu's gaze, Uju saw a reflection of her own desires and fears. It was as if they were two halves of a whole, incomplete without one another. The raindrops fell in rhythm with their heartbeat, a celestial dance that mirrored the unspoken passion between them.

Uju and Chinedu, their souls intertwined, made a silent vow to nurture this love that had blossomed in the rain. They knew that their journey together would not be without challenges.

Chapter 3: Trials and Tribulations

In the intricate dance of love, there are moments when the path becomes treacherous, and Uju and Chinedu found themselves navigating a landscape fraught with trials and tribulations. As rain poured from the heavens, mirroring the tumult within their hearts, they stood on the precipice of challenges that would test the strength of their bond.

Uju and Chinedu had always believed that their love was unbreakable—a force that could weather any storm. But as life unfolded, they encountered obstacles that shook the very foundation of their relationship. They found themselves entangled in a web of misunderstandings, external pressures, and the weight of their own expectations.

The raindrops tapped against the windowpane, like the echoes of their frustrations and doubts. Uju felt a growing sense of uncertainty—questions gnawing at her heart, threatening to unravel the love she held dear. She wondered if they were strong enough to withstand the trials that lay ahead, or if they were destined to succumb to the pressures that surrounded them.

Chinedu, too, grappled with his own inner turmoil. He felt the weight of the world on his shoulders—the relentless pursuit of his dreams, the demands of his career, and the fear of falling short. The rain outside matched the heaviness in his heart as he questioned his ability to be the partner Uju deserved, torn between his aspirations and the commitment they had made to one another.

In the face of adversity, Uju and Chinedu confronted their trials head-on, determined to find a way through the storm. They knew that love was not a smooth sail across calm waters but rather a voyage that required resilience, perseverance, and unwavering faith in one another.

They turned towards each other, seeking solace in the sanctuary of their love. They embraced the power of open communication, delving deep into their fears, insecurities, and desires.

Through tearful conversations and heartfelt vulnerability, they began to unravel the complexities that had entangled their hearts.

With every trial they faced, Uju and Chinedu discovered new dimensions of their love. They realized that true strength resided not in the absence of challenges, but in the way they faced them together. They learned to lean on each other, finding support and comfort in the understanding that they were not alone in their struggles.

As the rain continued to pour, their commitment to one another grew stronger. They made a pact—a promise to weather the storms that raged around them, hand in hand, heart to heart. They chose to view their trials as opportunities for growth, knowing that it was through overcoming obstacles that their love would be fortified.

Uju and Chinedu sought guidance from wise mentors and sought solace in the wisdom of those who had navigated similar paths. They surrounded themselves with a support system that lifted them up, providing guidance and encouragement when doubts threatened to overwhelm them.

They discovered the power of self-reflection—a sacred practice that allowed them to confront their own shortcomings and contribute to the healing of their relationship. They acknowledged their mistakes, taking responsibility for their actions, and committed to learning from the trials they faced.

With time, Uju and Chinedu began to witness the transformative power of their trials. They realized that their love was not defined by perfection but by their willingness to show up, to learn, and to grow. They understood that trials were not obstacles to be feared but steppingstones towards a love that was stronger, deeper, and more resilient.

As the rain gradually subsided, leaving behind a sense of renewal, Uju and Chinedu emerged from their trials with hearts that had been tempered by the flames of adversity. They saw the beauty that lay in their scars—the reminders of the battles they had fought and the strength they had discovered within themselves.

Uju and Chinedu held onto the lessons learned from their trials, knowing that their love had been tested and had emerged victorious. They faced the future with a renewed sense of hope, resilience, and a profound understanding that their trials had only strengthened the unbreakable bond they shared.

Together, they took a step forward, ready to face the challenges that awaited them. They knew that trials would continue to arise, but armed with the lessons of their past, they were prepared to navigate them with courage, compassion, and a love that had proven itself capable of overcoming the most formidable of obstacles.

"Whispered Promises: A Romantic Tale of Uju Uloaku"
Chapter 4: The Unveiling of Secrets

In the delicate tapestry of love, there often lie hidden threads of secrets, waiting to be unravelled. For Uju and Chinedu, the time had come for their souls to bear their deepest truths, to unveil the secrets that lay buried within the recesses of their hearts.

It was a tranquil evening, the air pregnant with anticipation as Uju and Chinedu found themselves nestled in the comfort of their shared space. The flickering candlelight cast dancing shadows on the walls, a tangible representation of the shadows that lingered within their souls.

Uju took a deep breath, the weight of her secret pressing against her chest. She investigated Chinedu's eyes, searching for the courage to share the truth that had haunted her for years. The vulnerability in his gaze assured her that this was a safe space, a sanctuary where their love could withstand even the harshest revelations.

"Chinedu," Uju began, her voice quivering slightly. "There's something I need to tell you, something I've kept hidden for far too long."

Chinedu, sensing the gravity of her words, took her hand in his, a gesture of reassurance and support. "Uju," he whispered, his voice a gentle balm to her restless soul. "You can trust me with your truth. Whatever it is, we will face it together."

With those words, Uju felt a wave of courage wash over her. She closed her eyes, gathering her thoughts, and then began to share the story that had remained locked within her heart.

"I was once in a relationship, a relationship that left scars upon my soul," Uju confessed, her voice heavy with the weight of past pain. "It was a relationship filled with manipulation and abuse, a time when I lost myself in the darkness of another's control."

Chinedu's grip tightened around her hand, a silent gesture of support and understanding.

"Whispered Promises: A Romantic Tale of Uju Uloaku"

Uju continued, her voice trembling but determined.

"I carried the burden of shame for years, believing that I was to blame for the wounds inflicted upon me," she confessed. "But through time and healing, I have come to realize that it was not my fault, that I am worthy of love and happiness."

Tears welled in Uju's eyes as the weight of her secret lifted, evaporating into the ether. Chinedu held her close, his embrace a shield against the pain that threatened to resurface. In that moment, Uju knew that her truth had found solace within the sanctuary of their love.

Chinedu, moved by Uju's vulnerability, felt compelled to share his own secret, to bare his soul in the same way she had done for him.

"Uju," he whispered, his voice filled with a mixture of regret and resignation. "There's something I need to tell you, something that has haunted me for years."

"Whispered Promises: A Romantic Tale of Uju Uloaku"

Uju leaned in, her eyes searching his, ready to receive the truth that lay within the depths of his being.

"I come from a broken family," Chinedu confessed, his voice tinged with sadness. "My parents' love was shattered by their own demons, leaving behind a legacy of pain and fractured relationships."

Uju's heart ached as she listened to Chinedu's revelation. She understood the weight he carried, the scars that marred his soul.

"I've spent years trying to mend the fragments of my fractured family," Chinedu continued, his voice filled with determination. "But the fear of repeating their mistakes, of not being enough, has haunted me. It's a battle I fight within myself every day."

Chapter 5: A Journey to Self-Discovery

The revelations of their hidden truths had laid bare the vulnerabilities of Uju and Chinedu's hearts. In the wake of their shared secrets, they found themselves embarking on a profound journey of self-discovery, each determined to heal the wounds of the past and forge a brighter future together.

Uju and Chinedu, united by their desire for growth and understanding, set out on a path of introspection and self-reflection. They understood that to build a strong foundation for their love, they needed to confront the remnants of their past and embrace the people they were becoming.

Uju, fuelled by a newfound strength, sought solace in the realm of self-discovery. She delved into the depths of her own psyche, exploring the layers of resilience that had carried her through the darkest days. Through therapy, journaling, and deep introspection, she began to unravel the intricate tapestry of her identity.

"Whispered Promises: A Romantic Tale of Uju Uloaku"

In the silence of her solitude, Uju confronted the scars of her previous relationship, unearthing the remnants of pain that had lingered within her. With each tear shed, she found the strength to release the shame that had bound her for far too long. It was a journey of healing, a reclamation of her worth and an affirmation that she was deserving of the love that bloomed between her and Chinedu.

Chinedu, too, embarked on his own quest for self-discovery. He sought solace in his music, allowing the melodies to guide him through the labyrinth of his emotions. The chords he strummed mirrored the complexities of his soul; each note an expression of the battles he fought within himself.

Through his lyrics, Chinedu began to unravel the layers of fear and uncertainty that had gripped his heart. He confronted the shadows of his fractured family, recognizing that he possessed the power to break the cycle of pain and forge a new legacy of love. His music became a vessel for transformation, a conduit through which he channelled his deepest emotions and aspirations.

Uju and Chinedu's individual journeys of self-discovery were intertwined, their paths converging as they sought to understand themselves and one another on a deeper level. They engaged in open and honest conversations, delving into the nuances of their fears, dreams, and the lessons they had learned along their separate journeys.

In each other's embrace, Uju and Chinedu found solace and strength. They became each other's pillars of support, their love acting as a guiding light as they navigated the uncharted territories of their inner worlds. They celebrated each other's victories, no matter how small, and offered a listening ear during moments of doubt and vulnerability.

Together, they explored avenues of growth and self-expression. They attended workshops and seminars, seeking wisdom from experts in various fields, eager to learn and expand their horizons. They indulged in literature, art, and music, nourishing their souls with the beauty and wisdom that the world had to offer.

In the process, Uju and Chinedu discovered that self-discovery was not a destination but a lifelong journey. They understood that growth required patience, compassion, and a willingness to confront their own limitations. As they grew individually, their love deepened, each layer of self-awareness adding richness and depth to their connection.

The journey of self-discovery revealed the intricacies of their souls, intertwining their paths in a dance of mutual understanding and acceptance. They realized that true love is not about finding someone who completes you, but rather finding someone who encourages you to complete yourself.

Chapter 6: The Power of Forgiveness

In the intricate tapestry of love, there exists a transformative power—a power that can mend even the deepest wounds and restore the broken pieces of the human heart. Uju and Chinedu, having weathered the storms of their relationship, discovered the incredible strength of forgiveness—a force that liberated their souls and paved the way for healing and renewal.

As raindrops fell softly against the windowpane, Uju and Chinedu stood on the precipice of a pivotal moment—a moment where the power of forgiveness would unfold before their very eyes. The weight of past hurts and misunderstandings had threatened to suffocate their love, but now, they were ready to embrace the liberating grace of forgiveness.

Uju, with tears streaming down her face, carried the weight of resentment within her heart. The scars of past betrayals had etched deep grooves in her soul, casting shadows upon the love she shared with Chinedu. The rain mirrored her tears, cleansing her spirit and beckoning her to release the burden that had burdened her for far too long.

Chinedu, too, carried the weight of guilt—a heavy burden that had cast a shadow on his self-worth. He longed for redemption, for the chance to make amends for the pain he had inflicted upon Uju. The raindrops mirrored his remorse, as if nature itself wept alongside him, longing for healing and reconciliation.

Together, Uju and Chinedu stood in the sacred space of vulnerability, baring their souls and acknowledging the pain that had kept them apart. They knew that forgiveness was not an easy path, but they also understood that it was a necessary one—a path that held the key to unlocking the shackles of their past and allowing their love to bloom once more.

In the quiet moments of reflection, Uju grappled with the complexities of forgiveness. She knew that forgiveness did not mean forgetting or condoning the pain she had endured, but rather releasing the grip of anger and resentment that had held her captive. The rain whispered a gentle reminder, encouraging her to open her heart and grant herself the freedom that forgiveness offered.

Chinedu, too, confronted the depths of his remorse. He yearned for Uju's forgiveness, but he also recognized the importance of forgiving himself—for only through self-forgiveness could he truly move forward and offer genuine remorse. The raindrops, like tears of absolution, bathed his soul, urging him to confront his past mistakes with courage and humility.

In the realm of forgiveness, Uju and Chinedu embarked on a journey of self-reflection. They delved into the depths of their emotions, exploring the wounds that had led to their pain and seeking to understand the underlying fears and insecurities that had fuelled their actions. Through introspection, they began to unravel the complexities of their hearts and the wounds that had shaped their relationship.

"Whispered Promises: A Romantic Tale of Uju Uloaku"

In the sanctuary of their love, Uju and Chinedu engaged in heartfelt conversations— conversations laced with vulnerability, empathy, and a genuine desire for understanding. They listened intently to each other's perspectives, acknowledging the pain they had caused and expressing remorse for their own shortcomings. Through open and honest dialogue, they began to bridge the chasm that had separated them.

With every word spoken and tear shed, forgiveness began to weave its transformative magic. Uju found strength in her ability to release the grip of resentment, allowing compassion and understanding to take its place. The raindrops that kissed her cheeks mirrored her inner transformation—a cleansing ritual that washed away the bitterness and made room for healing.

Chinedu, too, embraced the power of forgiveness, tenderly acknowledging the pain he had caused and offering sincere apologies. The raindrops that fell upon his outstretched palms symbolized his surrender—a surrender to the healing power of forgiveness, both given and received.

Together, Uju and Chinedu discovered the profound truth that forgiveness was not a one-time act, but rather a continuous journey—a journey of letting go, of embracing vulnerability, and of choosing love over resentment. They understood that forgiveness was not about erasing the past, but rather about rewriting the future—a future where their love could thrive and grow.

As the rain subsided, leaving behind a sense of cleansing renewal, Uju and Chinedu found solace in the embrace of forgiveness. They celebrated the beauty of their love—a love that had withstood the tests of time and emerged even stronger. In the depths of forgiveness, they found liberation—a liberation that allowed them to rewrite their story and cultivate a love that was rooted in compassion, understanding, and the power of second chances.

"Whispered Promises: A Romantic Tale of Uju Uloaku"

Together, Uju and Chinedu stepped into a future bathed in the light of forgiveness. They knew that challenges would continue to arise, but armed with the transformative power of forgiveness, they were prepared to face them with open hearts and a renewed commitment to nurturing their love.

Chapter 7: Amidst the Storm

Love, like life itself, is not immune to storms. Uju and Chinedu had come to understand that their journey together was not a smooth sail across calm waters but a voyage through tempestuous seas. In the face of adversity, they discovered the resilience of their love, the unyielding strength that would carry them through even the fiercest storms.

As the rain battered against the windows, Uju and Chinedu found themselves entangled in a web of challenges that tested the very foundation of their relationship. External pressures, insecurities, and the unpredictability of life threatened to cast dark shadows upon their love. They had to confront the question: could their love withstand the onslaught of the storm?

Uju faced professional setbacks—a project she had poured her heart into faced unforeseen obstacles, and doubts crept in, gnawing at her confidence. The weight of expectations bore down upon her, threatening to erode the passion that had once ignited her soul.

Chinedu, too, faced his own battles. His music career, though filled with moments of triumph, was fraught with uncertainty. The demands of the industry and the fear of failure whispered doubts into his ears, causing him to question the validity of his dreams.

During their individual storms, Uju and Chinedu turned to one another, seeking solace and reassurance. They became each other's anchor, offering unwavering support amidst the chaos that threatened to engulf them.

During sleepless nights, Uju and Chinedu shared whispered conversations, their voices carrying the weight of vulnerability and longing. They acknowledged the struggles they were facing and allowed themselves to feel the pain that accompanied those challenges. Their love became a safe haven—a shelter from the tempestuous winds that howled outside.

Together, they crafted a mantra—an affirmation of their commitment to weather the storm: "In the face of adversity, our love will not falter. We will hold each other's hand and navigate the tumultuous seas together."

Uju and Chinedu learned to communicate with unwavering honesty. They shared their fears and doubts, allowing vulnerability to deepen their connection. They listened, not only with their ears but with their hearts, offering understanding and empathy. In the darkest hours, they found solace in the simple act of being present for one another.

It was during a particularly turbulent night that their love was tested to its limits. The storm outside mirrored the tempest raging within their souls. Words, sharp as lightning, were exchanged, leaving wounds that threatened to scar.

Uju, overcome with frustration and exhaustion, questioned the very foundation of their love. "Is this storm too fierce to weather? Can we find our way back to each other amidst the chaos?"

Chinedu, his voice trembling with emotion, responded, "Our love is not fragile, Uju. It is fortified by the trials we face together. In the eye of the storm, we find the strength to rebuild."

In the aftermath of their heated exchange, Uju and Chinedu retreated into silence, each grappling with their own fears and insecurities. The rain poured down, its rhythm a mournful soundtrack to their hearts' struggle.

Days turned into nights, and as the storm outside subsided, so too did the storm within. Uju and Chinedu found themselves standing on the precipice of a choice—a choice to let the storm destroy what they had built or to rise stronger, fortified by the challenges they had faced.

With a renewed sense of purpose, Uju and Chinedu chose to rebuild, brick by brick. They extended forgiveness, offering understanding and compassion for the wounds inflicted in moments of vulnerability.

In the quiet of the night, Uju shared her letter with Chinedu. She read each word aloud, her voice quivering with a mixture of vulnerability and strength. Chinedu listened, his eyes brimming with tears as he witnessed the profound transformation taking place within Uju's soul.

Uju's act of forgiveness opened the floodgates for their shared healing. Chinedu, too, confronted the ghosts of his past—the shattered dynamics of his fractured family, the wounds that had festered in the recesses of his heart. With Uju by his side, he embarked on his own journey of forgiveness.

Together, they explored the power of empathy and understanding. They delved into the complexities of human nature, recognizing that everyone carried their own burdens, and that forgiveness was not an endorsement of the wrongs committed but a liberation from the chains of resentment.

They sought wisdom from spiritual leaders, psychologists, and writers who had studied the transformative nature of forgiveness. Through their research and conversations, they began to understand that forgiveness was not a one-time event but a continual choice—a process of healing and growth.

The rain outside mirrored the cleansing nature of forgiveness, washing away the remnants of pain and fostering new beginnings. Uju and Chinedu immersed themselves in rituals of forgiveness—meditation, prayer, and acts of kindness. They extended forgiveness not only to those who had hurt them but also to themselves, embracing their humanity and the imperfections that made them whole.

As they navigated the complexities of forgiveness, Uju and Chinedu found that their love became a sanctuary—a safe space where they could share their deepest wounds and support one another's healing. They celebrated each step forward, each moment of release, knowing that forgiveness was not a linear journey but a dance of resilience and grace.

Forgiveness became the bridge that connected their pasts with their present, allowing them to fully inhabit the present moment and embrace the possibilities that lay before them. They discovered that forgiveness was not a sign of weakness but a testament to their strength—the strength to choose love over bitterness, compassion over resentment.

In the forgiveness they bestowed upon one another, Uju and Chinedu found a love that was deeper and more profound than they had ever imagined.

Chapter 8: A Love Tested

Love is a flame that is tested in the crucible of life's trials. For Uju and Chinedu, their love had endured the gentle rain and the raging storms, but now they faced a new test—one that would challenge the very core of their commitment.

Life's unexpected turns had brought forth a wave of circumstances that threatened to pull them apart. Uju's career demanded her attention, pushing her towards new opportunities that required her to be away from Chinedu for extended periods. Distance, like a cruel mistress, whispered doubts into their hearts.

As Uju embarked on her professional journey, the space between them grew wider. Late nights turned into early mornings, and the moments they shared became fleeting, like whispers carried away by the wind. The physical distance weighed heavy on their hearts, as if an invisible barrier stood between them.

Chinedu, too, faced his own set of challenges. The demands of his music career intensified, requiring him to travel and dedicate countless hours to his craft. The pursuit of his dreams threatened to overshadow the connection he shared with Uju.

Amidst the chaos of their individual lives, doubts took root. In the quiet moments of solitude, they pondered the fragility of their love, questioning if the distance would slowly erode the foundation they had built. The pain of separation gnawed at their hearts, casting shadows upon the promises they had made to one another.

In the midst of their doubts, they sought solace in the power of communication. Uju and Chinedu embraced vulnerability, sharing their fears and insecurities, ensuring that their love was not overshadowed by unspoken emotions. They were determined to face this test head-on, together.

Late one evening, as rain cascaded from the heavens, Uju and Chinedu found themselves standing on the precipice of a difficult conversation. They knew that addressing their concerns was essential to preserving the bond they held so dear.

With trembling voices and hearts laid bare, they confronted the elephant in the room—the distance that threatened to pull them apart. They acknowledged the pain they felt, the longing that had become a constant companion.

"I miss you, Uju," Chinedu whispered, his voice tinged with longing. "The distance between us feels unbearable at times. But I refuse to let it overshadow the love we share."

Uju's eyes glistened with unshed tears as she nodded, her voice a delicate tremor. "I miss you too, Chinedu. The nights feel colder without you by my side. But I believe in us, in the love that has sustained us through every test."

Together, they crafted a plan—a roadmap to navigate the challenges that lay before them. They set aside dedicated time for communication, weaving virtual threads of connection to bridge the physical gap between them. Phone calls, video chats, and heartfelt messages became the lifeline that held their love together.

They also discovered the power of shared experiences, even from a distance. Uju and Chinedu watched movies together, synced their playlists, and found solace in the simple act of knowing that, despite the physical separation, their hearts beat in harmony.

In the face of their love being tested, Uju and Chinedu became warriors of hope, refusing to succumb to doubt. They drew strength from the foundation they had built, from the memories of the moments that had filled their hearts with joy.

Days turned into weeks, and weeks into months. With each passing moment, their love grew stronger, fortified by the trials they faced together. They learned that love, when tested, has the power to reveal its true essence—the

"Whispered Promises: A Romantic Tale of Uju Uloaku"

unwavering commitment to weather any storm.

Chapter 9: Healing Wounds, Mending Hearts

Love has the remarkable ability to heal the wounds that life inflicts upon our hearts. Uju and Chinedu, having weathered the tests and trials that came their way, now found themselves on a path of healing—a journey of tending to their scars, both old and new, and mending the tender fabric of their hearts.

As the rain washed away the remnants of a passing storm, Uju and Chinedu retreated to a place of solace—their shared sanctuary. They embraced the opportunity to nurture one another, to heal the wounds that had left their marks on their souls.

Uju carried the weight of past hurts—the scars from her previous relationship had etched themselves deep within her being. Though her love for Chinedu was unwavering, the echoes of the past occasionally resurfaced, casting shadows upon their present.

Chinedu, too, had his own battle wounds—emotional remnants of the fractured dynamics within his family that had left him questioning his own worthiness of love and stability.

In the quiet corners of their shared space, they turned towards one another, their eyes filled with compassion and understanding. They recognized that healing required patience, tenderness, and an unwavering commitment to one another's well-being.

Uju opened her heart, recounting the scars that had marked her past. With each word, she invited Chinedu into the depths of her vulnerability, knowing that he would hold her wounds with the gentlest of care. He listened, his presence a balm to her pain, assuring her that he was committed to walking alongside her on the path of healing.

Chinedu, in turn, shared his own struggles—the echoes of past trauma that had cast a shadow upon his ability to fully embrace love. Uju listened with unwavering empathy, offering him the space to heal and assuring him that he was deserving of the love they shared.

Together, Uju and Chinedu embarked on a journey of healing. They sought guidance from therapists, mentors, and spiritual guides, eager to shed light on the wounds that had shaped them. In each session, they unpacked the layers of pain and the habits that no longer served them, paving the way for transformation and growth.

They engaged in healing practices, both individually and together. Meditation became a sanctuary for stillness and self-reflection. Yoga allowed them to reconnect with their bodies, releasing tension and opening the pathways of energy within. Through journaling, they gave voice to their deepest emotions, allowing the ink to wash away the stains of the past.

In their exploration of healing modalities, they discovered the power of forgiveness. They extended forgiveness not only to others but also to themselves, recognizing that the wounds they carried were not their fault. Through forgiveness, they released the weight that had burdened their hearts, making space for love to thrive.

As they delved deeper into the healing process, Uju and Chinedu unearthed newfound compassion within themselves. They learned to hold space for each other's pain, offering support and understanding when old wounds resurfaced. Their love became a sanctuary—a place where healing was not only welcomed but nurtured.

Uju and Chinedu celebrated the small victories—a day without the echoes of the past haunting their minds, a moment of self-compassion that quelled the self-doubt. They celebrated each step forward, recognizing that healing was not linear but a dance of progress and setbacks.

In moments of vulnerability, Uju and Chinedu discovered the beauty of shared healing. They held each other's hands through tears and embraced one another in the warmth of unconditional love. They realized that healing, when nurtured within the container of their love, deepened their connection, and made them stronger.

Through their journey of healing, Uju and Chinedu learned that scars do not define them; rather, they are testaments to their resilience and capacity to love. They understood that the process of mending the wounds of the past is an ongoing journey, one that requires unwavering commitment and the willingness to face their shadows.

As the rain continued to pour outside, Uju and Chinedu sat in quiet reflection, their hearts intertwined. They were no longer defined by their scars, but rather by the strength and love that emerged from the process of healing. Their souls, once wounded, were now flourishing, radiating a renewed sense of wholeness and a deep appreciation for the transformative power of love and healing.

Chapter 10: Embracing the Unknown

In the tapestry of love, there are moments when the path ahead becomes obscured, and Uju and Chinedu found themselves standing at the threshold of the unknown. As the raindrops tapped against the windowpane, they contemplated the uncertainties that lay before them, their hearts a mix of anticipation and trepidation.

Uju and Chinedu had come to realize that love was not a linear journey with a predetermined destination. It was a dance with the unknown— a willingness to surrender to the twists and turns, the surprises and challenges that awaited them.

In the quiet moments of reflection, Uju found herself contemplating the future. Questions filled her mind: Where would their love lead them? What paths would they traverse together? And what would be required of them to navigate the uncharted territory ahead?

Chinedu, too, pondered the mysteries of the unknown. He understood that the road ahead was uncertain, but his heart swelled with a sense of adventure—a deep longing to explore the undiscovered facets of their love and to embrace the possibilities that awaited them.

Together, Uju and Chinedu made a conscious decision—to release their grip on the need for control and to embrace the beauty of surrender. They understood that in surrendering to the unknown, they would discover a profound sense of freedom and trust—a trust in themselves, in each other, and in the love that bound them.

As the rain continued to fall outside, Uju and Chinedu embarked on a journey of exploration. They sought to cultivate a spirit of curiosity, viewing the unknown not as a source of fear but as an opportunity for growth and discovery.

They allowed themselves to dream without limitations, envisioning a future in which their love would flourish amidst the uncertainty. They embraced the idea that the unknown held endless possibilities—a blank canvas upon which they could paint the vibrant strokes of their shared dreams.

With each step forward, Uju and Chinedu held hands, venturing into uncharted territory. They were aware that challenges might arise, but they faced them with resilience and an unwavering belief in their love. They understood that it was in the face of the unknown that their love would be tested and strengthened.

In the depths of their love, Uju and Chinedu nurtured a sense of openness—an openness to new experiences, new perspectives, and new dimensions of their connection. They sought wisdom from mentors and experts, immersing themselves in conversations that broadened their horizons and encouraged them to embrace the unfamiliar.

They took risks, knowing that growth often requires stepping outside of comfort zones. Uju pursued opportunities that stretched her boundaries, pushing herself to explore uncharted professional territories. Chinedu immersed himself in collaborations and musical endeavours that challenged his creative boundaries, allowing his talent to flourish in unanticipated ways.

As they journeyed into the unknown, Uju and Chinedu encountered moments of doubt and uncertainty. But in those moments, they leaned on each other, drawing strength from their shared commitment and unwavering support. They celebrated the triumphs, no matter how small, and found solace in the knowledge that they were navigating the unknown together.

Uju and Chinedu discovered that the unknown was not a void to be feared, but rather a canvas upon which they could paint their love story. They surrendered to the ebbs and flows of life, knowing that in embracing the unknown, they were embracing the beauty of possibility.

They learnt to cherish the present moment— the here and now that they had been gifted. During the rain-soaked days and starlit nights, they found joy in the simple pleasures—a

"Whispered Promises: A Romantic Tale of Uju Uloaku"

shared laughter, a gentle touch, and the knowledge that their love was a force that could transcend the uncertainties of the future.

Chapter 11: The Depths of Despair

In the labyrinth of love, there are moments when the depths of despair threaten to swallow even the most resilient souls. Uju and Chinedu found themselves navigating this treacherous terrain, where darkness overshadowed their once vibrant spirits. The rain fell relentlessly outside, mirroring the torrent of emotions that engulfed them.

Uju, burdened by the weight of her past, felt the tendrils of despair coil tightly around her heart. Memories of old wounds resurfaced, reminding her of the pain she had endured. Doubt clawed at her core, casting a shadow on the love she shared with Chinedu. Fear whispered venomous lies, causing her to question her worth and the possibility of finding lasting happiness.

Chinedu, too, wrestled with his own demons. The pursuit of his dreams seemed like an uphill battle, with obstacles lurking at every turn. Rejections and setbacks chipped away at his confidence, leaving him adrift in a sea of doubt and uncertainty. The weight of his struggles threatened to shatter the very foundation of his aspirations.

In the sanctuary of their shared space, Uju and Chinedu sought solace in each other's embrace. They clung to one another, their tears mingling with the raindrops that cascaded outside, seeking strength in their shared vulnerability. Together, they faced the darkness that threatened to consume them, determined to find a glimmer of light amidst the shadows.

They understood that despair was not a sign of weakness but a testament to their humanity—a raw and unfiltered expression of their deepest pain. In the depths of their sorrow, they discovered the resilience of their love—a love that refused to be extinguished by the darkness that surrounded them.

Uju and Chinedu reached out for support, seeking solace in the compassion of trusted confidants. Friends and family offered a comforting presence, a safe haven where they could unburden their hearts and find solace in shared experiences. In the embrace of loved ones, they found strength to face their inner demons and to hold onto the hope that lay dormant within their souls.

Within the depths of despair, Uju and Chinedu turned inward, engaging in a journey of self-exploration and introspection. They delved into the crevices of their hearts, peeling back the layers of pain to expose the wounds that lay hidden beneath. It was through this process of inner excavation that they began to understand the origins of their despair and the seeds of healing that resided within.

Uju and Chinedu embraced self-compassion, extending kindness and understanding to themselves in their darkest moments. They learned to hold space for their own pain and to nurture their wounded souls. In the depths of despair, they discovered the strength to be gentle with themselves, to forgive their own shortcomings, and to believe in their inherent worthiness of love and happiness.

They sought solace in creative expression—a refuge where their emotions could find release. Uju poured her heart into her writing, using words as a lifeline to navigate the labyrinth of her despair. Chinedu poured his emotions into his music, allowing the melodies to carry his pain and provide a cathartic release. Through their art, they discovered a channel for healing and a means of connecting with others who may be traversing similar depths.

Days turned into nights, and slowly, like a sliver of light piercing through stormy clouds, Uju and Chinedu began to glimpse moments of hope amidst their despair. They held onto these flickers of light, trusting that even in the depths of darkness, there was a path towards healing and renewal.

Together, they offered support and comfort, their love serving as a beacon of light in the face of despair. They celebrated small victories, no matter how insignificant they may have seemed—an act of self-care, a shared smile, a moment of respite from their burdens. In these fleeting moments of relief, they realized that their love was not defined by the depths of their despair, but rather by their unwavering commitment to support one another through the darkest of times.

As the rain gradually subsided outside, Uju and Chinedu clung to the promise of a brighter tomorrow. They understood that the depths of despair were not their final destination, but rather a crucible from which their love would emerge stronger and more resilient. Their hearts, though scarred, were filled with hope and the knowledge that love had the power to transcend even the most profound depths of despair.

"Whispered Promises: A Romantic Tale of Uju Uloaku"

Chapter 12: A Twist of Fate

In the tapestry of life, there are moments when fate intervenes, forever altering the course of our journey. Uju and Chinedu found themselves at the crossroads of destiny—a place where unforeseen circumstances conspired to reshape their lives and their love.

As the raindrops pattered against the windowpane, Uju and Chinedu stood on the precipice of change, their hearts a mix of anticipation and apprehension. Little did they know that a twist of fate was about to weave its way through their lives, forever changing their paths.

Uju had always believed in the power of serendipity—the notion that the universe had a way of orchestrating unexpected encounters and fortuitous moments. And it was during a chance encounter on a rainy evening that she met Ifeanyi, a charismatic and enigmatic individual who would leave an indelible mark on her life.

"Whispered Promises: A Romantic Tale of Uju Uloaku"

Ifeanyi was a stranger who seemed to possess an uncanny understanding of Uju's innermost desires and dreams. Their conversations flowed effortlessly, like a dance of souls entwined. Uju found herself captivated by Ifeanyi's charm and wisdom; drawn to the allure of a connection she had never experienced before.

As Uju navigated the complexities of her newfound bond with Ifeanyi, she couldn't help but question the implications for her relationship with Chinedu. Doubt gnawed at her heart, and she found herself torn between the familiarity and comfort of her love with Chinedu and the magnetic pull of this new connection.

Meanwhile, Chinedu felt an undercurrent of unease—an intangible shift in the dynamics of his relationship with Uju. He sensed that something was amiss, as if the winds of change were whispering secrets in his ear. His heart ached with uncertainty, and he longed for clarity amidst the tempest of emotions that swirled within him.

"Whispered Promises: A Romantic Tale of Uju Uloaku"

During their internal turmoil, Uju and Chinedu sought solace in each other's presence. They shared stolen moments of tenderness, desperately clinging to the fragments of their love that seemed to slip through their fingers like rainwater.

Uju, conflicted by the unexpected twist of fate, grappled with her emotions. She questioned the nature of her connection with Ifeanyi, attempting to reconcile the exhilaration she felt in his presence with the enduring love she shared with Chinedu. Her heart wavered, torn between the comfort of the familiar and the allure of the unknown.

Chinedu, sensing the growing distance between them, confronted Uju with his fears and vulnerability. He bared his soul, expressing the depths of his love and his desire to weather any storm that threatened to tear them apart. His voice trembled with emotion, and his eyes pleaded for reassurance in the face of uncertainty.

"Whispered Promises: A Romantic Tale of Uju Uloaku"

Uju listened, her heart heavy with the weight of her own doubts. The tears that streamed down her face mirrored the rainfall outside—a testament to the storm of emotions raging within her. In that moment, she realized that love was not a simple equation of logic, but a complex dance of the heart, guided by the whispers of fate.

In the depths of their shared conversation, Uju and Chinedu rediscovered the true essence of their connection—a bond forged through shared experiences, challenges, and triumphs. They understood that the twists of fate were not intended to tear them apart, but rather to test the strength of their love and commitment.

With hearts laid bare, Uju and Chinedu made a pact—a promise to navigate the uncertain terrain together. They acknowledged the allure of the twist of fate that had entered their lives, but they also recognized the depth of their love and the history they had built together. They chose to fight for their love, knowing that it was worth the struggle and the uncertainty that lay ahead.

As the rain subsided, leaving behind a glistening landscape, Uju and Chinedu embraced the unknown, hand in hand. They embarked on a journey of exploration and self-discovery, with a renewed determination to weather the twists and turns that fate had in store for them.

Little did they know that their love would be tested in ways they could never have imagined, and that the twist of fate would ultimately reveal the true depths of their hearts and the strength of their bond.

Chapter 13: The Strength of True Love

Love, when tested by the trials of life, has a remarkable ability to reveal its true strength. Uju and Chinedu, having navigated the twists and turns of fate, found themselves standing on the precipice of a profound realization—their love was forged in the fires of adversity, and it was unbreakable.

As the raindrops tapped against the windowpane, Uju and Chinedu stood side by side, their hearts intertwined. They had weathered storms and faced uncertainties, but through it all, their love had grown stronger, like a sturdy oak tree that withstood the fiercest winds.

Uju and Chinedu had come to understand that true love was not merely a fleeting emotion, but a profound commitment—an unwavering choice to stand by one another through the highs and lows of life's journey. Their love had endured, not because it was free from challenges, but precisely because it had been tested and proven resilient.

"Whispered Promises: A Romantic Tale of Uju Uloaku"

In the quiet moments of reflection, Uju marvelled at the depth of her love for Chinedu. She realized that their connection went far beyond mere infatuation—it was rooted in a profound understanding, acceptance, and unwavering support. Through every twist and turn, their love had remained steadfast, a beacon of light in the darkest of times.

Chinedu, too, found solace in the depth of their love. He cherished the moments of vulnerability they had shared, the tears they had shed, and the triumphs they had celebrated together. Their love was not defined by fleeting passion, but by a profound sense of companionship and a shared vision for the future.

As they reflected on their journey, Uju and Chinedu recognized that the strength of their love had been forged through the challenges they had faced. Each hurdle had tested their resolve, forcing them to confront their fears, communicate openly, and grow individually and as a couple.

"Whispered Promises: A Romantic Tale of Uju Uloaku"

Through the storms they had weathered, Uju and Chinedu had learned to lean on one another, drawing strength from their unwavering support. They had discovered the power of empathy, the art of truly listening, and the importance of being present for one another in both the joys and sorrows of life.

Their love was not without its flaws and imperfections, but it was precisely those imperfections that made it beautiful and authentic. They embraced the messy moments, the disagreements, and misunderstandings, knowing that true love was not about perfection, but about growth and forgiveness.

In the depths of their love, Uju and Chinedu found solace and stability. They realized that their love was not solely reliant on external circumstances, but on the unbreakable bond they had forged. It was a love that transcended distance, time, and the challenges that life presented.

They nurtured their love through daily acts of kindness and appreciation. They celebrated the small victories, cherished the shared laughter, and held onto each other tightly in moments of vulnerability. They understood that love was not a passive emotion, but an active choice—a choice to show up, to invest, and to prioritize their relationship.

As the rain outside gradually subsided, Uju and Chinedu made a pact—a promise to continue growing and evolving together. They acknowledged that their journey was not without its uncertainties, but they faced the future hand in hand, confident in the strength of their love.

Through the years that followed, Uju and Chinedu continued to embrace the lessons they had learned—the importance of communication, the power of forgiveness, and the beauty of unconditional love. They approached life's challenges with a sense of resilience and a deep trust in the foundation they had built.

Their love story became a testament to the strength of true love—a love that could

"Whispered Promises: A Romantic Tale of Uju Uloaku"

weather the fiercest storms and emerge stronger on the other side. Uju and Chinedu inspired those around them, a living testament to the power of unwavering commitment, genuine connection, and the strength of the human heart.

As they looked towards the horizon, Uju and Chinedu knew that their love would continue to evolve, grow, and be tested. But they were confident that if they faced life together, hand in hand, their love would endure—a beacon of hope and strength in a world that often seemed chaotic and uncertain.

Chapter 14: Redemption and Second Chances

In the vast tapestry of love, there is a thread that weaves redemption and second chances— a transformative power that can breathe new life into even the most broken of souls. Uju and Chinedu, having navigated their fair share of challenges, found themselves at a crossroads— a moment where the possibility of redemption and the gift of second chances beckoned.

As the rain washed away the remnants of the past, Uju and Chinedu stood on the threshold of a new chapter in their lives. They had traversed through storms of despair, embraced the unknown, and tested the strength of their love. And now, in the dawning light, they realized that redemption was within their grasp.

Uju, haunted by the ghosts of her past, carried the weight of regrets and mistakes. She longed for a chance to make amends, to heal the wounds she had inflicted upon herself and others. The raindrops mirrored her tears as she sought forgiveness, not only from those she had hurt but also from herself.

Chinedu, too, carried the burden of past actions—choices he regretted, words he wished he could take back. He yearned for the opportunity to grow, to become a better version of himself. The raindrops washed away the stains of his past, offering a chance for renewal and redemption.

Together, Uju and Chinedu embraced the power of redemption. They understood that it required humility, self-reflection, and the willingness to confront the shadows within. They embarked on a journey of self-forgiveness, seeking to mend the broken pieces of their souls and find solace in the embrace of second chances.

Uju reached out to those she had hurt, offering sincere apologies, and seeking understanding. She engaged in deep introspection, confronting the patterns and beliefs that had led her astray. Through therapy and self-exploration, she began to understand the roots of her actions and to heal the wounds that had driven her to hurt others.

Chinedu, too, took responsibility for his past mistakes. He sought to make amends, not only through words but through actions that demonstrated his growth and commitment to change. He immersed himself in personal development, devouring books, attending workshops, and seeking guidance from mentors who could help him become the person he aspired to be.

As the rain continued to fall, Uju and Chinedu found solace in their shared journey of redemption. They supported each other through the ups and downs, providing a safe space for vulnerability and growth. Together, they recognized that redemption was not a solitary pursuit but a collective effort—a journey they would undertake side by side.

They embraced the power of second chances— a gift that allowed them to rewrite their stories and create a brighter future. They let go of the shackles of past mistakes, knowing that dwelling in guilt and regret served no purpose. Instead, they focused on the present moment and the possibilities it held.

Uju and Chinedu embarked on a mission to rebuild trust—both in themselves and in their relationship. They understood that trust was not easily regained but required consistent effort and transparency. They committed to open communication, honest conversations, and a willingness to confront their fears and insecurities head-on.

In their pursuit of redemption, Uju and Chinedu discovered the power of self-love and self-compassion. They forgave themselves for their past shortcomings, recognizing that growth and transformation were continuous processes. They embraced the notion that their past did not define them, but rather served as a catalyst for their evolution.

As the rain gradually subsided, Uju and Chinedu found themselves basking in the warmth of newfound redemption. They understood that redemption did not erase the past but offered a path towards healing and renewal. They allowed themselves to be guided by the lessons learned from their mistakes, using them as steppingstones towards a brighter future.

Their love, once tested and strained, became a testament to the power of redemption and second chances. They nurtured their relationship with tenderness and patience, celebrating the growth they witnessed in each other. They knew that true redemption was not a destination but a lifelong journey—an ongoing commitment to embrace the beauty of forgiveness and growth.

As Uju and Chinedu looked towards the horizon, they embraced the uncertainties that lay ahead with newfound strength and hope. They understood that redemption was not a one-time event but a daily practice—a choice to show up, to learn from their mistakes, and to cultivate a love that was grounded in compassion and forgiveness.

Together, they embarked on the next chapter of their lives—a chapter infused with the

"Whispered Promises: A Romantic Tale of Uju Uloaku"

transformative power of redemption and the gift of second chances. They walked hand in hand, their hearts overflowing with gratitude for the opportunity to rewrite their story and create a love that would stand the test of time.

Chapter 15: Forever in Each Other's Arms

In the realm of love, there exists a sacred space—a place where souls intertwine, and hearts find solace. For Uju and Chinedu, that sacred space was nestled in the embrace of each other's arms—a haven of comfort, acceptance, and eternal devotion.

As the raindrops danced upon the windowpane, Uju and Chinedu stood before their future, their hearts overflowing with a love that had weathered storms and grown stronger with each passing day. They had traversed the depths of despair, embraced the twists of fate, and found redemption in their journey together.

Uju and Chinedu had come to realize that true love was not a fairytale ending, but rather a lifelong commitment—an unbreakable bond that transcended the boundaries of time and space. Their love was built on a foundation of trust, mutual respect, and unwavering support—a sanctuary in which their souls found sanctuary.

"Whispered Promises: A Romantic Tale of Uju Uloaku"

In the quiet moments of reflection, Uju felt the warmth of Chinedu's embrace enveloping her, like a protective shield against the world's uncertainties. His touch ignited a flame within her, a flame that burned with passion, tenderness, and unwavering devotion. In his arms, she found solace—a sanctuary where she could be her most authentic self.

Chinedu, too, cherished the sacredness of their embrace. Uju's presence was a balm to his soul—a constant reminder that he was seen, heard, and deeply loved. Her touch awakened a profound sense of belonging within him, a sense that he had found his forever home in the curve of her arms.

As they stood together, raindrops tracing pathways down the window, Uju and Chinedu marvelled at the journey they had embarked upon. They had witnessed the depths of each other's vulnerabilities, the intricacies of their dreams, and the resilience of their love. They understood that their bond was not without challenges, but it was precisely those challenges that had forged their connection, transforming it into a love that could withstand the tests of time.

Uju and Chinedu shared a language of touch—a gentle caress, a hand intertwined with another, and a tight embrace that spoke volumes of their affection. In the tenderness of their touch, they found solace and reassurance—a reminder that they were not alone in this vast world, but forever connected, heart to heart.

Through the highs and lows of life, Uju and Chinedu promised to be each other's pillars of strength. They celebrated the triumphs with exuberance, lifting each other higher with joyous laughter and shared victories. In moments of sorrow, they embraced one another, providing solace through silent understanding and the power of their unwavering love.

Together, Uju and Chinedu created a sanctuary—a space where vulnerability was celebrated, where tears were embraced, and where dreams were nurtured. They understood that true intimacy was not solely physical, but also an emotional connection that allowed them to delve into the depths of their souls and discover the essence of their being.

Their love was a refuge, a sanctuary that shielded them from the chaos of the world. In each other's arms, they found solace from the burdens of life, a respite from the noise and uncertainty that surrounded them. Their embrace was a testament to the power of love—the power to heal, to uplift, and to provide a sense of belonging that transcended all boundaries.

As the rain gradually faded away, leaving behind a serene ambiance, Uju and Chinedu took a vow—a vow to navigate life's twists and turns hand in hand, heart in heart. They understood that their love was not a destination, but a continuous journey—a journey in which they would grow, evolve, and continue to find solace in the sacred embrace of each other's arms.

"Whispered Promises: A Romantic Tale of Uju Uloaku"

Their love story, marked by the trials and triumphs they had faced together, was a testament to the beauty of enduring love. They had discovered that love, when nurtured with tenderness and devotion, had the power to create a haven—a haven where they would forever find solace, joy, and the sweet assurance that they were meant to spend eternity in each other's arms.

"Whispered Promises: A Romantic Tale of Uju Uloaku"

Epilogue

In the realm of love, where stories are woven and destinies are shaped, Uju and Chinedu's journey had been one of triumph, resilience, and unwavering commitment. As the rain subsided, leaving behind a gentle mist, they found themselves standing on the precipice of a new chapter—a chapter that celebrated the depths of their love and the growth they had experienced.

Through the twists and turns of their relationship, Uju and Chinedu had discovered the transformative power of forgiveness, the strength that emerged from trials and tribulations, and the unwavering support they found in each other's arms. Their love had weathered storms that threatened to tear them apart, but it had emerged even stronger forged in the fires of adversity and enriched by the lessons they had learned along the way.

As they looked back on their journey, they were reminded of the beauty of second chances— the chance to rewrite their story and create a love that defied the odds. They had navigated the labyrinth of self-discovery, faced their deepest fears, and embraced the unknown. In doing so, they had found within themselves a wellspring of resilience and the capacity to love unconditionally.

Uju had blossomed into a woman who embraced her own worth—an individual who understood the power of vulnerability, forgiveness, and self-compassion. Her words had become a tapestry of emotions, weaving stories that touched the hearts of those who read them. She had discovered her voice, her purpose, and a love for herself that radiated outwards, enriching the lives of those around her.

Chinedu had embarked on a journey of personal growth, honing his talents, and channelling his passion into his music. His melodies carried the weight of his experiences—the trials, the depths of despair, and the triumphs that shaped his path. Through his art, he had found solace, connection, and a

"Whispered Promises: A Romantic Tale of Uju Uloaku"

means to inspire others to embrace their own unique journeys.

Together, Uju and Chinedu had built a love that defied the limitations of time and space. Their bond was a testament to the power of forgiveness, resilience, and the unbreakable thread of destiny that had woven their lives together. They had faced the depths of despair, embraced the unknown, and emerged with hearts that were more open, compassionate, and resilient.

As they stood on the cusp of their future, Uju and Chinedu knew that their journey was far from over. They understood that love, like life itself, was a continuous evolution—a tapestry of joy, pain, growth, and transformation. They faced the unknown with a newfound sense of adventure, eager to explore the uncharted territories that lay before them.

Their love story would continue to unfold—a symphony of emotions, challenges, and moments of profound connection. They would face new trials and tribulations, but armed with the wisdom gained from their past, they were ready to face whatever lay ahead.

As the rain gave way to the warmth of sunlight, Uju and Chinedu walked hand in hand, their hearts entwined. They knew that their love had stood the test of time—a love that was anchored in forgiveness, resilience, and a deep understanding of one another. They carried with them the lessons learned, the scars that told stories of growth, and a love that would forever be etched in their souls.

And so, their love story continued—an ever-unfolding narrative of redemption, second chances, and the boundless power of a love that defied all odds. With hearts filled with gratitude, they embraced the beauty of their journey—a journey that would forever be inscribed in the annals of their hearts, a testament to the indomitable spirit of love and the infinite capacity of the human heart to heal, to grow, and to love unconditionally.

"Whispered Promises: A Romantic Tale of Uju Uloaku"

Appreciation

I am thrilled to announce the completion of my book. This journey has been a testament to perseverance, dedication, and the power of words. But this accomplishment would not have been possible without your unwavering support and love.

To my sister, Gege & BB your encouragement has been a beacon of light in moments of doubt. Your belief in my abilities pushed me to transcend boundaries and strive for excellence.

To my mother, your unconditional love and wisdom have been my guiding force. You taught me the value of hard work and the importance of staying true to my vision.

And to my children, you are my greatest inspiration. Your curiosity, joy, and innocence remind me of the wonders of life and the importance of capturing them in words.

This book is not just a reflection of my thoughts and experiences, but also a tribute to you all. Your roles in my life have shaped my perspectives, which have found their way into the pages of this book.

Thank you for being a part of this incredible journey. This accomplishment is as much yours as it is mine.

With deepest gratitude and love.

Printed by Amazon Italia Logistica S.r.l.
Torrazza Piemonte (TO), Italy

53775389R00051